I Could Pee on This

AND OTHER POEMS BY CATS

I Could Pee on This

AND OTHER POEMS BY CATS

BY FRANCESCO MARCIULIANO

CHRONICLE BOOKS

SAN FRANCISCO

Library of Congress Cataloging-in-Publication Data
Marciuliano, Francesco.
  I could pee on this, and other poems by cats / by Francesco Marciuliano.
    p. cm.
  ISBN 978-1-4521-1058-5
  1. Cats—Poetry. I. Title.

PS3613.A7348C68 2012
811'.6—dc23
                2011053152

The following images copyright © iStockphoto.com/photographer: Joseph Luoman, 2 (type-
writer); David Meharey, 2, 42 (mouse); sansara, 6; Oleg Prikhodko, 10–11; Anita Bonita, 13,
91; 1001slide, 14; Ary6, 19; Peterfactors, 20; Dave Long, 22 (passport); dyachenko, 22 (kitten);
Maria Pavlova, 26; Loran Nicolas, 27; S. W Krull Imaging, 28; Eric's Photo Lab, 33; fotoja-
godka, 34; Nailia Schwarz, 38; Viktor Kitaykin, 41; bibikoff, 45; Chris Leachman, 47; knape,
48; Spurious2, 50; ktaylorg, 55; Mehmet Torlak, 57; kimeveruss, 58; spooh, 60; DOConnell,
62–63; prill, 64; deemac, 67; Ben Heys, 68; PK-Photos, 70; Aptyp_kok, 73; Cheramie Photo,
77; Dixi_,78; TheFingerS, 80; Chic Type, 82; Watcha, 84; ATesevich, 86–87; herreid14, 93;
Peeter Viisimaa, 94; skynesher, 102; kevinjeon00, 94; Serg Petrov, 109 (kitten); fcdb, 109
(stamp); spxChrome, 110. The following image copyright © Shutterstock.com/photographer:
foaloce, 101. 4–5 copyright © Francesco Marciuliano, 17 © George Shuklin via Wikimedia
Commons, 36–37 copyright © 2007–2009 texturez.com—All Rights Reserved. Frame images
copyright © 2010 www.free-photo-frames.com—All Rights Reserved, excluding frame images
on pages 19, 33, 55, 77, 105, and 109

Manufactured in China

Designed by EMILY DUBIN

40 39 38 37 36 35 34 33 32

Chronicle Books
680 Second Street
San Francisco, California 94107
www.chroniclebooks.com

MIX
Paper from
responsible sources
FSC
www.fsc.org   FSC™ C136333

Dedicated in loving memory to
Boris and Natasha,
two unforgettable cats
who I had the great fortune
to call family

CONTENTS

INTRODUCTION

For thousands of years, cats have strived to express to humans what it means to be feline. They have tried body language, plaintive meowing, even a filmmaking style best described as "fallen camera nudged across floor until forgotten or smeared with saliva." And for thousands of years, we humans have witnessed this unending struggle for true emotional and spiritual connection and said, "Wook at that wittle furry face! Wook at that wittle furry face! Who's got a wittle furry face? You've got a wittle furry face!"

But now, through the power of poetry and a publishing contract, cats everywhere can fully welcome people into their hearts, minds, and souls. Within these very pages, you'll find poems penned by cats that reveal their every desire, their every conflict, and their every epiphany. You'll also discover why cats do things like put their whole paw in your glass and then look at you as if you've never had a date over for wine before. Seriously, their whole paw. Like they think it's easy to get cabernet out of orange tabby.

In fact, by the time you've finished reading this poetry anthology, you'll not only completely understand everything your cat thinks and does but even applaud him for it. Maybe give him a medal. Or throw him a parade in your hallway, making sure to avoid staircases so all the tiny floats don't tumble down. Or you can just sit your cat down, look him straight in the eyes and say, "I get it. I really do get it . . . furry face."

From the litterbox of . . .

FAMILY

Sometimes when I lie on your warm chest

And hear your every happy sigh

I gaze into your two kind eyes

And wonder, "Who is that?"

CAT EPIGRAM

I COULD PEE ON THIS

Her new sweater doesn't smell of me
I could pee on that
She's gone out for the day and
  left her laptop on the counter
I could pee on that
Her new boyfriend just pushed
  my head away
I could pee on him
She's ignoring me ignoring her
I could pee everywhere
She's making up for it
  by putting me on her lap
I could pee on this
I could pee on this

I LICK YOUR NOSE

I lick your nose

I lick your nose again

I drag my claws down your eyelids

Oh, you're up? Feed me

CLOSED DOOR

LET ME IN LET ME IN LET ME IN
LET ME IN LET ME IN LET ME IN
LET ME IN LET ME IN LET ME IN
LET ME IN LET ME IN LET ME IN
LET ME IN LET ME I—

Oh, uh, hello

I did not expect an answer

I did not expect an entrance

I did not expect this room to be
  so unbelievably dull

So, uh, goodbye

WHY ARE YOU SCREAMING?

Why are you screaming?

What did I do wrong?

Why are you crying?

How can I make it right?

Would you like it in a different color?

Would you like it in a different size?

Would you like it in a different room?

I just wanted to show my love

I just wanted to express my thanks

I just wanted to put a dead mouse

  on your sheets

But now you are screaming

And I don't know how to make you stop

WHO IS THAT ON YOUR LAP?

There's another cat in the house
A cat I've never seen
A much *younger* cat
You seem to know her name
You accidentally called me by her name
Right in front of the lamp
And my friend the throw pillow
I've never been so humiliated
I may never love again

SEPARATION

You can have the CDs,

  I will take the string

You can have the TV,

  I will take this fuzzy thing

You can have the kitchen set,

  I will take this crumpled foil

You can have the car,

  I will keep this rug I soil

You can have the beach house,

  I will take this tissue box

You can have everything,

  Ooo I want those dirty socks

You can go to hell, I will see to that

For how dare you come home

  smelling of another cat?

SOMETHING'S WRONG

Something's wrong
Why are the walls a different color?
Something's not right
When did we get these stairs?
Something's off
How did the kitchen move across the floor?
Something's going on
Who changed all the homes outside?
Something's very odd
Why are you mispronouncing "Georgia"
  as "New York"?
Something happened
When you put me in that carrying case
And someday soon
I will figure it out

UNBRIDLED LOVE

I knead your chest with my sharp claws

To show you my affection

I bite your arm and don't let go

To show you adoration

I walk across your throat at night

Because I want to say, "Hello!"

I leap from high upon your crotch

Because I miss you so

I trip you when you walk down the stairs

So you know I'm always near

I sit on your face and block all your air

So my absence you need not fear

I show my love in so many ways

My devotion runneth over

So I don't know why when I approach

You duck and run for cover

BROTHERS

They say we are brothers though
  we look nothing alike
They say we are family though
  we differ so much
I am tabby, you are brown
I am long, you are short
I am thin, you are stout
I am lively, you are shy
I am a kitten, you are a hamster
But kin is kin
So let me run on your wheel

Meowy Christmas!

FROM OUR LITTER TO YOURS

O CHRISTMAS TREE

O please

O come on

O like you didn't know

What you were getting for Christmas

Before I ripped open all your gifts

O by the way

The tree looks better on its side

O I really do think so

THE LEASH

Don't put that thing around my neck
Don't take me out the front door
Don't show me off in the park
Don't drag me into every store
Don't smile when people stop and stare
Don't sit outside and talk on the phone
Don't walk me all over this damn town
Then wonder why you're still alone

SERIOUSLY

Seriously?

Seriously?!

SERIOUSLY?!

If I took YOU to the doctor

I would make damn sure

You came back with both of them

Down there

Now if you'll excuse me

I'm going to look forlornly out a window

For like eighteen years

Eighteen loooooooooong years

Seriously?!

FOREVER

I could lie by your side for the rest
  of our lives
I think I'll walk away right now
I could let you pet me for
  a hundred years
I think we need some time apart
I could be kissed a thousand
  thousand times
I think I'm needed somewhere else
I could sit on your lap forever
I said I could sit on your lap *forever*
Don't you even think of trying to get up
Well, you should have gone
  to the bathroom beforehand
Because forever is a very, very long time

THIS IS MY CHAIR

This is my chair

This is my couch

That is my bed

That is my bench

There is my chaise

There is my settee

Those are my footstools

Those are my rugs

Everywhere is my place to sleep

Perhaps you should just get a hotel room

MY LIFE IS RUINED

That was just for you
That was just our little joke
So we could share a little laugh
Just the two of us alone
But you took that special moment
You posted it online
Now forty million people think
I bark like a dog
And so I hide under the covers
Cursing your very name
Saying you better get a good lawyer
Or me a great agent

CHAPTER

2

WORK

They say there are
Twenty-four hours in a day
But I'm only up for three of them
And two I consider overtime

CAT PROVERB

I LICK

I lick my neck, I lick my chest
I lick my back to look my best
I lick my paw to wash my face
I lift my leg to lick that place
I lick my tail, I lick my belly
I lick my back or did I do that already?
I lick my tail, maybe once more
Oh what the hell, let's make it four
I lick my neck in case I forgot
Did I lick my chest? Well, I missed a spot
I lick my face, my leg, my tail, my face
I relick my belly and then, yes, my face
I lick all the time, I'm so soil-free
Seems the only thing I can't lick is my OCD

YOUR KEYBOARD

Suetdhe8defdisjas

I just typed a poem in your presentation

Chsothekstevdswdj

I just typed a joke in your email

Nosyd76mhdlwdag

I just typed something personal

  on your update

Vos7swps8s73wbk

I just typed my political views

  in your tweet

Bhst9ahw-2ynsyhz

I just accidentally typed in

  your bank account password

Kitty's gonna buy himself

  a new scratching post

catbook 🐱 💬 🌐   Search

ℹ️ Meows

📷 Photos (32)

ONE DAY

One day words I shall talk
One day on my hind legs I shall walk
One day your books I shall read
One day I shall dress in your finest tweed
And on that day when I talk and walk
When I know the facts
  and look stunning in slacks
When I am your equal
  and not under your command
I shall stride right up and fully demand,
"Can you get my favorite fuzzy toy
  from under the bed?
It's been there for like a week,
  and I can't reach it"

BUSY, BUSY

It's 8 A.M. and time to rest

It's 10 A.M. and time to relax

It's noon and time for repose

It's 3 P.M. and time for shut-eye

It's 6 P.M. and time for siesta

It's 9 P.M. and time to slumber

It's midnight and time to snooze

It's 4 A.M. and time to hang upside down
  from your bedroom ceiling, screaming

SCRATCH

Scratch Scratch Scratch
Scratch Scratch Scratch
Scratch Scratch
Scratch

There
It is done
Now gaze upon your sofa leg
And see an exact replica
of Rodin's *The Thinker*

I mean, if you look at it
from just the right angle
Anyway, on to my next masterpiece—
Turning your curtains into confetti

Really, I should have
my own gallery show

TALK TO ME

Tell me about your day
Tell me about your dreams
Tell me about the girl you adore
The one who smiles but walks away

Tell me your greatest fears
Tell me your biggest secrets
Tell me your most cherished moments
The ones that light your darkest days

Tell me why things don't work out
Tell me why stuff gets in the way
Tell me why it stops you cold
The one thought you can't let go

Lie on the couch and talk to me
Open your mind and bare yourself
Because I think I finally figured out
  how to bill you
And I'm about to make a fortune

DID YOU KNOW

Did you know?

Did you see?

Did you count?

How many times

I had to smack that moth

On your forehead

With my paw?

It was like a thousand

He's dead now, though

Definitely dead

One more smack

You're welcome

NINE LIVES

The first life is for running

The second life is for staring

The third life is for climbing

The fourth life is for tearing

The fifth life is for sleeping

The sixth life is for sleeping

The seventh life is for sleeping

The eighth life is for sleeping

The ninth life is for writing my memoirs

I RUN

I run across the room
I race across the floor
I dash to this wall
I thought I saw something
I forgot what it was
Now everyone is staring at me
So I run back across the room
I race back across the floor
I dash back to that other wall
So everyone will think

  I'm just running laps

TRIPPED.

I'm sorry I tripped you in the hall
I'm sorry I tripped you in the den
I'm sorry I tripped you in the bedroom
I'm sorry I tripped you in the kitchen
I'm sorry I tripped you in the attic
I'm sorry I tripped you in the basement
I'm sorry I tripped you out the door
I'm sorry I tripped you on hard cement
But some men paid me five grand to kill you

WE'RE ALL IN THIS
TOGETHER

I cleaned the floor

With your sweater back and forth

I cleared the table

With a few whips of my tail

I dusted your shelves

Of all the knickknacks you kept

I made your bed

Smell a lot more like me

I'm here to help

I want to do my part

After all, we're all in this together

CALL ME

You can

Call me

"Muffins"

All you want

But 'til

You add

"Sir"

At the start

I'm not turning my head

CHICKEN AND RICE

Chicken and rice for the first day
Chicken and rice for the second day
Chicken and rice for the third day
Chicken and rice for the fourth day
Chicken and rice for the fifth day
Chicken and rice for the sixth day
Lamb and rice today
And just like that my world crumbles

AND NOW WE KNOW

Nine-hundred-and-ninety-five
I'm doing this for you
Nine-hundred-and-ninety-six
So please don't interrupt
Nine-hundred-and-ninety-seven
I'm just keeping them honest
Nine-hundred-and-ninety-eight
So please do take note
Nine-hundred-and-ninety-nine
And now thanks to me we all know
There really were one thousand sheets
  in this toilet paper roll

KNEEL BEFORE ME

In ancient Egypt

We cats were gods

We ruled the heavens

We reigned on earth

So kneel before me

I said come to me

Uh, listen to me

How about just a treat then?

Okay, maybe a toy

Some crumpled paper would do

I'm not picky

Well, can you at least scratch

  behind my ear?

Can you at least do that?

Oh

Oh yes

You serve your master well

CHAPTER

③

PLAY

Life is a hallway

Meant to be explored

One barely head-sized hole at a time

CAT ADAGE

NUDGE

Nudge

Nudge nudge nudge

Nudge nudge nudge nudge nudge nudge

Nudge

Your glass just shattered on the floor

TINY BOXES

Tiny boxes

Play and hide

Tiny boxes

Squeeze inside

Tiny boxes

Cozy here

Tiny boxes

Paw in ear

Tiny boxes

Stuck

STUCK

STUCK!!!

Tiny boxes

Little help?

KITTEN

HOLY [censored], THAT BALL CAN BOUNCE!
GET THE [deleted] OUT OF HERE,
  THIS STRING IS GREAT!
SON OF A [removed], I CAN RUN SO FAST!
NO [banned] WAY, I JUST BROKE THAT PLATE!
WHAT THE [edited], DID YOU SEE ME JUMP?!
WELL [forbidden] ME, I'M CAUGHT IN A JAR
MOTHER [bleep], I SHOWED THAT LAMP!
OH [cut] NO, THERE GOES YOUR GUITAR!
UN-[denied]-BELIEVABLE,
  I CAN CLIMB YOUR LEGS!
NO [blocked] LIE,
  I CAN DISTRESS YOUR FLOOR!
FOR [erased] SAKES, ISN'T MY LIFE GRAND?!
SO [censored] SAD I'M A KITTEN
  FOR JUST SIX MONTHS MORE!

SOME OF MY BEST
FRIENDS ARE DOGS

Some of my best friends are dogs
We talk about dog things
Some of my cat friends don't get it
We laugh at their fear
The dogs see me as one of their own
True, they don't like it when I bark
Or play dead
Or chew their toys
Or sniff their butts
But we're cool
Some of my best friends are dogs
I just thought you should know

THEN ALL WENT DARK

I'M BLIND!

Oh wait, I'm not

I'M BLIND!

No, my vision is clear

I'M BLIND!

But now I see you

I'M BLIND!

And there you are again.

I'M BLIND!

What is going . . . Wait,

  is that your hand over my eyes?

THAT TOP SHELF

I think I can jump to that top shelf
I want to jump to that top shelf
I *know* I can jump to that top shelf
I am jumping to that top shelf
I missed that top shelf by a good six feet
And now everything is on the floor
And I'm left wondering
Why people even bother buying china
If it breaks so easily

THE WORLD
OUTSIDE MY HOUSE

In the world outside my house
The mice jump in your mouth
And birds serve themselves in butter
Rather than fly south

In the world outside my house
The sun is a laser light
Each cloud a snuggly blanket
And the doors are not shut tight

In the world outside my house
All the trees they dangle string
The flowers brush from head to tail
And the neutered cat is king

In the world outside my house
I can never go
But as an indoor cat I know these things
Because the dog does tell me so

MOST AMUSING

HAHAHAHAHAHAHAHA

HAHAHAHAHAHAHAHA

Hahahahahahahaha

Haha Haha Ha

That dog is wearing a sweater

MY TAIL

If my tail is curved then I am at ease
If it is tucked then do what you please
If it twitches then get out of my sight
If it is to one side then I'm free for the night
If it is fluffed then I simply can't deal
If it swishes then it's about to get real
If it is erect then for you I give thanks
If it is gone then I'm probably Manx
If it grabs food then you're petting a monkey

You should probably walk away right now

ELEGY FOR A
TOY I BROKE

You no longer jingle

You no longer roll

You no longer do anything

Since I had to see what made you work

I can't deal with all this guilt

I can't express my deep, deep grief

I can't believe what a cheap piece of
 crap you were

Seriously, I hardly touched you before
 you broke

MEOW

Meow

Meow meow meow

Meow meow

Meow meow MEOW!

Well?

Why aren't you laughing?

Sigh

I must have told the joke wrong

SUSHI

Did you really think
That you could hide fish in rice?
Oh, the green paste burns!

A CAT LIKE ME

I didn't know you had a second sofa
I didn't know you had a second TV
I didn't know you had a second cat
One who looks just like me

I didn't know you had another living room
I didn't know you decorated it just the same
I don't like this twin cat
  staring back at me
Well, two can play at that game

I don't know why I can't get into
  that other living room
I try and try but can't get through
I don't know why you yell at me
  not to scratch the mirror
When that twin cat is doing it, too

THIS. WILL. NEVER. END.

It's been four days since we started
It's been three days since you ate
It's been two days since your boss called
And fired you for being late
But you're the one who did this
The one who put the feather on the string
The one who waved it for me to play
The one who made my heart just sing
So welcome to your eternity

KUBLA KAT

On the edge of a laughing teacup
Did Kubla Kat decree
That the corn fritter festooned with medals
Shall make the brownies free
And so the walls turned to water
To let our sorrows drown
As the chairs burned themselves for warmth
So they need not face the clown
Then the spoons burst into song
And all the forks they understood
As I stared at my now talking claws
Because this catnip is just that good

EXISTENCE

Everything I do you hate

Is pure instinct

Everything I do you love

Is pure me

CAT APHORISM

SELF-AFFIRMATION

I am intelligent

I am attractive

I am powerful

I am proactive

I have value

I have health

I have strength

I have stealth

I am surrounded by love

I am a beacon of hope

I—HORKFLAKGLORKSPUKE

. . .

That was a hairball

And I am a cat

And what just happened

I am fine with that

NATURE'S WAY

The leaf twirls gently
  to the dry ground
The flake tumbles lightly
  to the snowy mound
The lightning falls mightily
  to the earth with a crash
And I plummet sleepily
  from the fridge to the trash.
Such is nature's way

JUST THE TWO OF US

There is nothing like long

Direct

Intense

Awkward

Unfortunate

Eye contact

To help us see

That maybe you put my litter box

Too close to your favorite chair

I'M NOT PARANOID

I'm not touching my food because
  there's a pill in it
I'm not having that treat because
  there's a pill in it
I'm not going near your hand because
  there's a pill in it
I'm not playing with that toy because
  there's a pill in it
I'm not going into that room because
  there's a pill in it
I'm not sleeping on that couch because
  there's a pill in it
I'm not looking at the sky because
  there's a pill up there
I'm not doing anything because
  there's a pill everywhere

You may think I'm paranoid

You may think I'm rather nuts

But you're not going to fool me twice

And besides, I think I can cure

  hookworm with my mind

GIVE

You can't hold someone who
  wants to leave
You can't clutch a memory
  as if it were today
You can't take an insult
  close to heart
You can't grasp for glory
  from your chair
You can't seize life
  thinking only of loss
And you can't grab a laser pointer dot
  on the wall
No matter how much you try
These hard-earned truths I give to you

SIAMESE

What's the longest you can hum
  before they say you've gone insane?
What's the difference between a street,
  an avenue, and a lane?
Have you ever told an ethnic joke
  and insulted a nearby ghost?
Have you ever wondered what happened
  to "Happy Days" star Donny Most?
If a hurricane were named "Mortimer,"
  would anyone run away?
If a toaster were brought to life,
  would it clean its own crumb tray?
Why don't leprechauns use their gold
  to pay off their student loans?
Why don't ninjas ever forget
  to silence their cell phones?

I know many people think
  that Siamese are way too chatty
I know they all think we just
  talk and talk and talk
But you're wide awake in bed
  just staring at the ceiling
So maybe you could tell me
  why not whiteboard and black chalk?

COLD

This table is cold
That hand is cold
The needle is cold
The stethoscope is cold
The doctor is cold
The nurse is cold
This room is cold
The only thing that's warm
Is the puddle of urine
   I made on the vet's notes

EVERYONE

Everyone has restless leg syndrome
Everyone has slipped, or fell
Everyone suffers from depression
And bladder dysfunction as well
Everyone should sue their doctor
Everyone can't sleep at night
Everyone can't do the simplest task
When filmed in black and white
Everyone must buy insurance
Everyone owes the taxman pay
Everything looks so bleak and hopeless
Since you left the TV on
   to keep me company all day

BIGGER CAT

I'm not fat, I'm big-boned

I'm not fat, I'm a bigger breed

I'm not fat, it's just more hair

I'm not fat, it's just more muscle

I'm not fat, it's only winter weight

I'm not fat, it's only a trick of the eye

I'm not the reason you threw out your back

But the next time you lift me,

  do so with your knees

NECTAR OF THE GODS

Lap, lap, lap
Savor the oak
Lick, lick, lick
The sweet fruit delights
Slurp, slurp, slurp
So delicate in structure
Gulp, gulp, gulp
So complex in nature
Oh, I didn't know water
  could taste like this
Oh, I didn't know the sink faucet
  was such bliss
Oh, I can't believe all those years
  I did piss
Away drinking that swill you serve
  in my bowl

I'M SO MAD I COULD—

What do you think you—
How could you treat me like—
Don't you dare turn on that—
Oh hell it's torture in all this—
AUGH! AUGH! It's going in my—
How could you do such a cruel—
Don't you dare put me in—
I'm going to kill you right—
Let me just scratch your eye with my—
Stop interrupting me with your—
Will this nightmare ever—
Oh, it's over

Okay then

But this is the last time
   you're ever giving me a bath

N O

I know what "No" means

I know what you said

I know you said "No"

I heard you every time

I know you screamed, "Don't break it"

I know you shouted, "Don't do that,
  you hear?"

But I don't know why

You're upset it's now broken

When I know for a fact

You didn't say, "No don't do that"

The seventh time I smacked it

When your head was turned

MAN'S BEST FRIEND

Why is the dog man's best friend?
Because I don't greet you at the door?
Because I don't wave my tail when you leave?
Because I don't play catch or fetch?
Because I don't do a single trick?
Because I don't beg for your attention?
Because I don't answer when you call?
Well, I also don't watch you having sex
And let's just say the dog talks

I MISS ME

I miss my special sunny place
I miss my head pressed against your face
I miss the carpet rub against my paws
I miss the sofa tug at my claws
I miss skidding across the kitchen floor
I miss yowling at your bedroom door
I miss lying on my windowsill
I miss refusing to take my pill
I miss my family, my home, your sweater
I even miss that worthless Irish Setter
I miss everything that once was me
Before I climbed this stupid tree

CUTE BED JUMP

Cute bed jump
See yes yes
No don't door
Ball ball couch
Yes chin ear
Got tail tail
Run food skid
I'm just three
Weeks old and
Not good with
Man talk yet

ACKNOWLEDGMENTS

My deepest thanks to Emily Haynes, Scott Mendel, Emily Dubin, Becca Cohen, Emilie Sandoz and the fantastic people at Chronicle Books who made all this possible and let me keep the word "Pee" in the title.

And a very loud "Thank You!" for all the love and support from Mom, Dad, Marcello, Kim Lofgren, Ari Jaffe, Lena Verkhovsky, Maryanne Ventrice, Dan Piraro, "Alspaugh" and every cat who somehow managed to use a keyboard without typing "Thustewje cdtfxjhsyt kshs" for 120 pages.

FRANCESCO MARCIULIANO writes the comic strip *Sally Forth*, which runs in 700 newspapers (and the webcomic *Medium Large*, which does not). He was Head Writer for the Emmy Award-winning children's show *SeeMore's Playhouse* and has written for *Onion News Network*, *Smosh.com*, *McSweeneys*, and The New York International Fringe Festival. It took him over 30 years to learn how to spell his entire name correctly.